My Heart Song

Published by Inspire Books
www.inspire-books.com

Architect's Daughter font used by permission.
Shutterstock images used by permission

ISBN: 978-1-950685-21-9 paperback
ISBN: 978-1-950685-22-6 hardcover
Library of Congress:

Printed in the United States

My Heart Song

Written by Shillann Rodriguez-Peña

Illustrated by Bri-Anne Kitka

For my daughter, Rian.
You have taught me more in
five years than many learn in a lifetime.
The impact you have on others is powerful.
Keep shining your light and I will do my very
best to help you share it with the world.
Mommy loves you more than you know.

Xo

If I could reach all the stars in the bright night sky, I would take a few just for you.

We'd have a bucket
full of wishes
of whatever
you choose . . .
and I'd make
sure they
all came
true.

If I could fly around the world,
I'd have you there with me and
above the clouds we'd soar.

I'd show you all the beauty
of the things we'd see
that you never knew before.

3

If I could own a boat,
It'd be a great big ship-
we'd be the captains,
you and I.

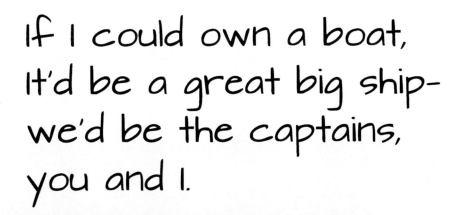

We would sail the seven seas
as we feel the ocean breeze
leave our worries all behind.

'Cause your smile's like the rainbow that takes away the grey.

And the sparkle
in your eyes
shines brighter
than the light
of day.

The sound of your laugh
warms my soul
more than words
could ever say.

8

Of all the things
in all the world,
I'm so glad
we have today.

And from today, all the way,
'till forever more, my love,
I'll be with you.

Up the mountains, through the valleys and the streams in between . . . wherever life takes us to.

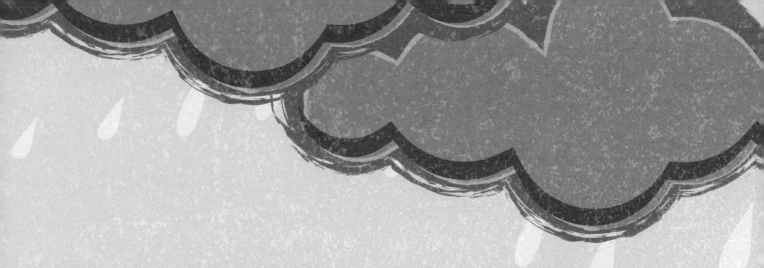

And when the clouds of life roll in
and things begin to change,
please know my love
will stay the same.

It'll just be you and I,
underneath the stormy sky,
as we're dancing in the rain.

13

'Cause my love for you
is stronger than our sun
that shares its rays.
And like the stars we wish
upon, my love is here
to stay.

14

So don't you ever wonder
if my love will go away.
Because it's true
my love for you
grows bigger
every day.

15

won- der if my love will go a- way Be-

cause it's true my love for you grows big- ger ev- ery day

To listen to an audio file of this heartwarming song, please visit the My Heart Song Book YouTube channel at this URL: http://bit.ly/YouTubemyheartsong

My Heart Song

How This Book Came to Be

Dear Parent/Adult Readers,

Our daughter, Rian (who just turned five years old at the time of publishing this book) lives with a rare, life threatening disease called AADC deficiency. In a very condensed explanation, this condition affects every aspect of her life and results in complete disruption of her motor function. Because of this, Rian has yet to meet any motor milestones that typically happen during infancy and beyond. Despite the incredible toll her disease has taken on her, she is a very smart girl. She uses smiles and eye movement to communicate with us and the world around her. She is also very aware of how much she is loved and just how much she means to us.

During Rian's first year of life, I really wanted to buy a book that I could read to her and have it be our "special book," just as I did with her older brother. Typically, this would not be a difficult feat, but every book I looked at served as a constant reminder of all the things she couldn't do. The imagery in the books that I found depicted babies and young children sitting on their own, reaching for a hug or clapping their hands—all things that I so desperately wanted her to experience but she couldn't.

I could not bear to read her books with imagery that was so unrelatable, and it brought me to tears every time.

Eventually, I connected with local support groups for parents with children who have additional needs. One day I asked if anyone had some suggestions as to a suitable book for us. I received many great responses, however the suggestions were books that showed pictures of children using wheelchairs and walkers—supports that Rian was not yet using and truthfully, at the time, those too were images that brought tears to my eyes.

I couldn't believe how incredibly difficult it was to find a book that suited us!

One night, before her first birthday, I was putting her to bed and had just finished singing the lullaby that I wrote for her. While she was falling asleep, I was thinking of how much I wished we had a special book to read before bed and said to her:

"When are we ever going to find a book for US??"

At that moment I came to the realization that I already had a "book" for us—it was just in the form of a song! I became excited to think how the lullaby I wrote for her IS our story.

From that night on, I had the vision of creating this book, not just for Rian, but for other children and families who may be in similar situations. Families who, like us, face differences but don't always want to be reminded of them. Families who would like to curl up and enjoy the simplicity of reading a book with their child and not think about their hardships. Families like us who, above all else, just want to feel like they belong.

The imagery in this book has been mindfully created to not highlight any of the children's abilities or lack thereof. Simple design and solid colours have been used in hopes to help children with visual processing challenges more easily see and enjoy its pages. Every child pictured in this book is supported, in one way or another, by a loving adult.

The mission of this book is to make ALL readers feel that its words and images apply to them. Whether the readers are families with typically developing children or children with additional needs, the message is simple—never-ending, constant love. Something that ALL families who purchase this book can relate to.

This book is very dear and personal to me. The words captured on its pages have been sung from my heart to Rian's ears for years now. Whether it's been while comforting her after surgery, calming her during hospitals stays, or as I help her fall asleep in the comfort of our home, Rian knows that these words hold my promise of always being there for her.

The musical component of this book is something I love! The hybrid of story and song is something I haven't seen in children's books, and I am so happy to be able to deliver this to you. It provides a unique opportunity for people to sing its words and/or play its melody to their own child, just as I have sung it to Rian, oh-so-many times.

Lastly, and certainly not least, I would like you to know that all proceeds will be donated to The AADC Research Trust—the only charity in the world dedicated to AADCd. Funds will be used to directly impact the lives of children around the world, like Rian, affected by AADC deficiency. Life enhancing and life saving technologies are increasingly attainable and on the rise for AADCd. I would like you to know that by buying this book, you are contributing to spreading help and hope on a global scale.

Thank you so much. I hope this book provides you with the opportunity to share special moments reading and/or singing to your loved child because, after all, in this life, it's those moments that mean so very much.

From the bottom of My Heart Song,

Shillann Rodriguez-Peña

For more information on The AADC Trust, please visit: https://www.aadcresearch.org.
On social media and interested in learning more about life with AADCd?
Please check out:
#RaisingRian, #CureAADC, #CureAADCd

AADCd Families from Around the World Captured in This Book

Page 6: Hallie with mom, Lucy
England

Page 8: Jamell with mom, Shante
U.S.A.

Page 13: Rian and mom, Shillann
Canada

Page 14: Anna with mom, Stephanie
Austria

The Importance of the Dragonflies

When your child has a life-limiting condition, you must come to the realization that time may not always be on their side. Of the approximately 130 children worldwide living with AADCd, we have lost 23 children within the last 4 years alone. I have paid tribute to them, as well as all of the other medically fragile children we have met on our journey who have passed away, by including a dragonfly on each image in this book.

The dragonfly is affectionately known as a symbol of hope after death, reminding us that passing on is not an end, but a transformation. It was important for me to honour the memory of these children—because they matter. Their presence remains as they live on in our hearts and through each and every illustration in this book.

Until we meet again . . .

Thanks & Acknowledgments

There have been so many wonderful people involved in the creating of My Heart Song, and I am so grateful to have had them all be a part of it.

Thank you to Inspire Books, who graciously waived all book production costs to contribute towards my mission of supporting The AADC Research Trust. Inspire Books has been happy to take on this important role, knowing that it will help children and fund potentially life-saving and disease-transforming treatments. I am forever grateful for their help, guidance, and generosity with *My Heart Song*. Thank you for believing in the importance of this book, in its message of inclusion, and for seeing how it will bring joy to the many families who read it.

To my good friend, Bri-Anne. Since the beginning of our journey with AADC deficiency, you have been such a wonderful support in SO many ways. Thank you for volunteering your time and remarkable talent to this project—it means so much to me. You have done a phenomenal job of mindfully creating these beautiful and inclusive illustrations. Your work will touch the hearts of many who will see themselves through your images. You are awesome, and I am blessed to call you my friend.

To Timothy Smith of Lowe's School of Music, thank you for bringing "My Heart Song" to life by capturing its sound on sheet music. You have made my dream of sharing its melody a reality, and working with you was such a delight. Thank you for all of your patience and support during the process—it is so very appreciated.

25

To my dear childhood friend, Jill Barber. For some time, I have daydreamed about having a recording of "My Heart Song" sung by your beautiful and unique voice. I truly cannot express in words how happy I am that this has come to fruition! I can only imagine how busy it must be, balancing your successful singer-songwriter career along with family life, raising two young children. The fact that you so willingly accepted my ask for your involvement really touches my heart. Thank you for making this project a priority and for completely volunteering your time & talent—it means so much to me and speaks volumes of your character. Thank you for being my voice and for helping me share this little song of mine—your incredible talent is only matched by the kindness you hold in your heart.

Last, but nowhere near least, I would like to thank my husband, Mike. Thank you for your unwavering support throughout the creation process of *My Heart Song* and for all that you do for our family. You never expect a thank you, but you always deserve one. You love our children with an equal amount of intensity, despite their many differences. You step up like a hero to what many would turn away from, and you love our children harder than any father I know. Thank you for loving us and for always being the rock to which we anchor our family. No matter how turbulent the winds of life become, your strength and stability always reminds us that, with you, we can get through any storm.

About the Author

Since her own childhood, **Shillann Rodriguez-Peña** has had a love for creating songs and poetry. Once she became a mother, this love easily adapted itself to writing lullabies and songs for her children. *My Heart Song* is Shillann's first published book, but it won't be her last! With a professional background in social services, she has always had a heart for helping others. Her love for humanitarianism and her unique blend of song and story shine through in this project, as she is dedicating all proceeds to The AADC Research Trust, an incredible charity that is very dear to her heart. Shillann lives just outside of Toronto, Canada, with her husband Mike and their young children, Jonah and Rian. Her daughter Rian (pictured here with Shillann) is the reason why this book came to be, and is the strongest person Shillann has ever known.

About the Illustrator

Bri-Anne Kitka is a graphic designer who lives and works just outside of Toronto, Canada. She and her boyfriend Jake adore being parents to their seven-year-old son Johnny who keeps their hearts full of love and their house filled with laughter. She was approached by Shillann, a long-time friend, to illustrate this unique book and loved the idea that it was a project to benefit charity. She jumped at the opportunity and eagerly took on a new but very special challenge—illustration. Bri-Anne has volunteered her time and talent free of charge to this project. She has enjoyed applying her artistic abilities to *My Heart Song* as she finds fulfillment in knowing that her work is contributing not only to The AADC Research Trust but also to the lives of the families that find belonging in her images.

Manufactured by Amazon.ca
Bolton, ON